Pamela loves pi... so much she eats it ... breakfast. She is a ... mechanic who can f... about any motor she gets her paws on.

PAULINA is shy and loves to read about faraway places. But she loves traveling to those places even more.

Nicky is from the Australian Outback, where she developed a love of nature and the environment. This outdoors-loving mouse is always on the move.

Thea Sisters

HELLO! WELCOME TO THE FABUMOUSE WORLD OF THE THEA SISTERS!

Thea Sisters

Hi, I'm Thea Stilton, Geronimo Stilton's sister! I am a special reporter for _The Rodent's Gazette_, the most famous newspaper on Mouse Island. I love traveling and meeting new mice all over the world, like the Thea Sisters. These five friends have helped me out with my adventures. Let me introduce you to these fabumouse young mice!

Colette has a real passion for fashion. She loves to design her own clothes in her favorite color, pink.

Violet loves studying and learning new things. She is a fan of classical music and dreams of becoming a famous violinist someday.

Thea Stilton

MOUSEFORD ACADEMY

MOUSELETS IN DANGER

Scholastic Inc.

ISBN 978-0-545-67011-1

Text by Thea Stilton
Original title *Tea sisters in pericolo!*
Cover by Giuseppe Facciotto
Illustrations by Barbara Pellizzari (inks) and Davide Turotti (color)
Graphics by Yuko Egusa

Special thanks to Beth Dunfey
Translated by Lidia Morson Tramontozzi
Interior design by Kevin Callahan / BNGO Books

12 11 10 9 8 7 6 5 4 3 2 1   14 15 16 17 18 19/0

Printed in the U.S.A.   40
First printing, September 2014

STRANGE SPRING BREEZES

It was early spring on Whale Island, and a **STRONG WIND** had been gusting for a few days. The gale had swept away the clouds, and a bright spring sun was shining in the clear blue sky.

Despite the nice weather, Ruby Flashyfur was in a stormy mood. The rivalry between Ruby and the Thea Sisters was getting more tempestuous by the hour.

For months now, Ruby had been plotting to make the Thea Sisters look bad, but so far the

mouselets had foiled all her plans. Ruby was intent on REVENGE.

"I'll find a way to get those GOODY TWO-PAWS mice!" she told her friends Alicia, Connie, and Zoe—the Ruby Crew. "I just need the RIGHT opportunity."

She got her chance just a few days later. The morning's first ferry arrived with a special guest on board. He was a devoted sportsmouse covered in MUSCLES. And his name was *Bruce Hyena*!

At the suggestion of Thea Stilton, Mouseford Academy's visiting professor of adventure journalism, Headmaster Octavius de Mousus had invited Bruce to give a series of **special** lectures at the school.

"My most adventurous students need a course in **SURVIVAL TECHNIQUES**," Thea had told the headmaster, "and I know the perfect teacher. Bruce and my brother Geronimo climbed Mount Kilimanjaro together. He's the **perfect** mouse for the job!"

MR. TORNADO

Bruce scrambled off the ferry, took a deep breath of fresh AIR, and began scampering toward Mouseford Academy.

He reached campus in the blink of a cat's eye. It was still early, and classes had not yet begun. The most ATHLETIC students, like Nicky and Craig, were outside exercising.

"Good for you, young cheese puffs!" Bruce **bellowed**. "First train your frame, then train your brain!" He started giving the students advice on the best way to exercise.

"Come on, move those paws!" Bruce squeaked. "Hup, hup, hup! SPRING from the ankles when you jump rope!" Bruce demonstrated his own personal technique.

Passing students were ATTRACTED

to Bruce's impromptu lesson. Soon a crowd of young rodents had gathered around him.

"Look sharp, all of you! And don't forget to stretch for better flexibility!" Bruce told them. He rotated his torso from side to side. "See, cheese puffs? Twist like a TORNADO!"

The headmaster scurried over to see what was going on. When he recognized Bruce, his snout broke into a wide **GRIN**. He shook Bruce's paw vigorously.

"welcome to Mouseford Academy!"

Then the headmaster turned to the students and added, "Don't miss Professor Hyena's presentation at ten o'clock in the auditorium. We'll explain the course and collect your registration cards then. See you all later!"

The headmaster took Bruce by the paw and led him into the main office.

Word of the *dynamic* new teacher spread across campus faster than the smell of melting cheese. Within half an hour, the students had chosen the perfect nickname for him: **MR. TORNADO**!

SURVIVAL COURSE

By nine thirty, the school auditorium was brimming with **BUZZING** students. Craig was the most **excited** about the new teacher. "This rodent seems like a real he-mouse. With a coach like him, we'll lock up the **BASEBALL** championship this year, and maybe the annual Rodents' Regatta, too!"

"The way you're squeaking, this guy must be a magician," Shen SNORTED. "Our boat is so old, it's practically PREHISTORIC! We'll need a miracle to win the regatta."

There was a lot of **curiosity** from other students, too. Ruby was no sports fan, but she'd already taken her place in the front row.

"You never know what might happen," she

said to her crew, smiling SHREWDLY. "We might actually learn something from this musclemouse!"

At ten o'clock SHARP, Bruce strode into the room. "Hey there, young cheese puffs! I'm here to turn you into real **ADVENTURE MICE**!"

The Thea Sisters beamed at him. But Ruby just **WRINKLED** her nose. "Humph! He's such a cavemouse!"

The headmaster SCURRIED to catch up with Bruce, stopping to catch his breath. "Professor Hyena is famouse throughout the world for his **extreme adventures**! He will be teaching a course on survival techniques. His class will last six weeks, and it's open to everyone."

Bruce adjusted his trademark mirrored *sunglasses* and inspected the students before him. "Who here knows how to work **HARD**? I see lots of promise, but only if you're ready to work your paws off. If you exercise both your *bodies* and your BRAINS, you'll be tough enough to climb Mount Kilimanjaro if you want to!"

The mouselets in the audience smiled up at him.

"No **WORRIES**, young rodents," continued Bruce. "I'll teach you how to face the fiery dunes of the *desert* and the snowy **blizzards** of the North Pole. By the end of my class, you'll all be thanking me while you work out, or my name isn't Bruce Hyena!"

Professor Hyena had squeaked only briefly, but the students leaving the auditorium were absolutely in **awe** of him.

What a cool mouse!

"He's so energetic, and he seems super smart, too!" remarked Paulina.

Violet nodded. "I was afraid his class would be just for jocks, but he makes it sound like quick wits are just as important as big muscles! I'm going to sign up. How about you?"

"Of course," Nicky said. "We'll all sign up!"

"Yes! Let's do it, sisters," cheered Pamela.

The mouselets turned to Colette, who generally hated any activity that might mess up her fur-do. To their surprise, she agreed immediately.

"Are you kidding me? Professor Hyena is cooler than cottage cheese! Plus, he's friends with Thea. Of course we have to sign up!"

LET'S MOVE IT, YOUNG CHEESE PUFFS!

Practically every mouselet at the academy **SIGNED UP** for Professor Hyena's course. Bruce decided to hold his LESSONS early in the morning, out on the campus grounds. His motto was: *"An active mouse is a happy mouse!"*

He liked to use funny slogans to motivate his students. They **giggled** as Bruce led them through his famouse exercise regimen, squeaking words of encouragement:

"No **LAZY** mice here, only crazy mice — crazy for *fitness*!"

"You can do it! Slow but steady, tired but inspired!"

"Come on, work those paws! HUP, HUP, HUP! You can thank me later!"

Professor Hyena led his class UP and DOWN the wooded areas surrounding the academy. He wanted the students to enjoy the BEAUTY of nature as he demonstrated real-world survival skills.

First, Bruce taught them how to MAKE

sturdy knots. Next, he showed them how to climb trees to see the terrain around them. Then he explained the difference between an edible mushroom and a POISONOUS one.

Pamela was super impressed with Bruce. "He's **FASCINATING**! I can't imagine a boring class with Professor Hyena."

For Nicky, Bruce was the ideal trainer. "It's so inspiring to see an athlete who believes in pursuing his own dream," she declared. "He's a scampering, squeaking example for us all!"

The other Thea Sisters enjoyed Professor Hyena's lessons, too — each for a different reason. Paulina APPRECIATED his

knowledge of nature. "He's always teaching us new and useful things, but best of all, he's showing us paws-on ways to respect the environment."

"That's so true," agreed Colette. "And these brisk walks give me so much energy!"

Violet had discovered a little secret about the new professor. "He loves POETRY just as much as sports. Look at this beautiful book he lent me!"

Not all the students admired Bruce as much as the Thea Sisters. Ruby found his lessons tedious. "This stuff went out with the CAVEMICE! With today's technology, everything is done a lot quicker and better."

"If that's how you feel, then why did you

tell us to sign up?" asked Connie, **perplexed**.

"Because the Thea Sisters signed up," sighed Ruby. "I thought we'd learn some good workout techniques, so we could get in shape. But instead I'm about to fall asleep. This musclemouse is more boring than a trip to Ho-Hum Island . . . all we're doing is TRAMPING around!"

The only member of Ruby's crew who was truly interested was Zoe, and she had her own secret agenda: She had a **CRUSH** on Craig! Since he was excited about the course, Zoe didn't want to miss a single session. Too bad Craig was so **ABSORBED** in Bruce's lessons, he didn't even notice her!

A CONTEST
ON THE HORIZON

After weeks of fitness training and survival instruction, Bruce decided to put his students to the **test**.

"I'm thinking of a survival contest, with the mouselings pairing off in groups of two," he explained to the **HEADMASTER**. "Two days in the woods should be long enough for them to practice the concepts they've learned."

The headmaster was a little **DUBIOUS**. "Hmmm . . . what exactly will the students have to do?"

"Survive!" Bruce replied. To him, it was the most **obvious** thing in the world. "They'll build their own shelters and find their own food and drink. **No** comfy feather

beds! **No** fancy cheese sandwiches! **No** hot showers!"

The headmaster blinked again. "Why in pairs?" he asked.

"**COLLABORATION** is very important," explained Bruce. "My goal is for the mouselings to learn to work together in *harmony*, with respect for **nature**!"

The headmaster was impressed with Bruce's mission. "Excellent! These are fundamental lessons for our students. When the contest is complete, they can each write an **ESSAY** about their experience," he said. "I'll look for a **MAGAZINE** willing to publish the best essay."

Bruce nodded. "Sounds like a plan!"

Bruce had already *explored* Whale Island and selected the best place for the survival challenge: the Forest of Hawks. He unrolled a **MAP** on the headmaster's desk.

"Every team needs to be completely independent — on their own, in their own **space**. I've explored the forest, and I estimate that no more than

Here's the place!

TWELVE students will be able to participate."

When the contest was announced on the school's bulletin board, Bruce's students went into a fur-flying frenzy!

Nicky ran to tell her friends. "The contest is only open to **SIX** pairs! We ab-so-lu-te-ly have to sign up first!"

Colette didn't look so sure. "Well, I don't know —"

Pam cut her off before she could finish squeaking. "You can *TEAM UP* with me, Colette. It'll be fun! Come on, let's shake a tail!"

Zoe was excited about the contest, too. She scurried to Ruby's room, but soon found that her friend was MOODIER than a muskrat. She was preoccupied with a BROKEN pawnail. And when Zoe explained they'd be spending two days in the **woods**,

Ruby was horror-struck.

"I've had it up to my whiskers with that CAVEMOUSE! No way am I going to ruin my manicure for a stupid contest no one will participate in anyway!"

But Zoe refused to be **discouraged**. This contest was her chance to get Craig to notice her, and she was determined to make the most of it.

A COLDHEARTED
CAVEMOUSE

By the next morning, Mouseford Academy's students were more excited than a pack of mouselings at Ratty Potter World. All twelve **contest** slots were filled in record time.

Everyone waited ANXIOUSLY to be assigned their places in the woods. The Thea

It'll be fun!

Sisters had been the first to reach the sign-up sheet, so they were all selected to participate.

Ruby was beginning to have second thoughts about not entering the contest. Her classmates were so **enthusiastic** that she was feeling a little **left out**. Her doubt turned to certainty when Zoe confessed that not only had she signed up, but she'd also convinced Alicia to be her partner!

The Thea Sisters will do their best to win, Ruby thought bitterly. *They'll be more popular than Cheesy Chews, and I won't be able to do a thing about it!*

So she scurried off to find Professor Hyena. He was in the kitchen **CHATTING** with the cook, Midge.

"Thanks, some whole wheat muffins and scrambled eggs are just what I need to put **FUR** on my chest! I just swam around Whale

Island and I want to **recharge** the old batteries."

"Professor Hyena," Ruby interrupted, "I want to sign up for the contest!"

Bruce's whiskers *quivered* with annoyance. He was a strong believer in punctuality. And he absolutely hated being interrupted.

I want to sign up for the contest!

"Negative!" he said firmly. "Enrollment is closed. The deadline has passed."

Ruby stamped her PAWS on the floor. "I DE-MAND to have a chance!"

Bruce shrugged. "I repeat, the deadline has passed. When I give a deadline, it's for real, and that's nothing to sneeze at!"

One of the Thea Sisters' FRIENDS, Elly Squid, happened to be passing the kitchen as this little scene took place. She was on her way to meet the mouselets, and she told them what she'd seen.

"Wow!" giggled Pam. "Sounds like the professor really put her in her place."

"Yes, and he left her just standing there with her tail between her paws!" Elly said, laughing. "Ruby was **redder** than a golden hamster!"

"Serves her right," said Colette. "Maybe

she'll learn she can't always **BOSS** everyone around."

But Paulina shook her snout. "I doubt it. There are certain things Ruby will **NEVER** learn. She's probably calling her mommy right now!"

Paulina was right. At that very moment, Ruby was on her *phone*, screeching at her mother, Rebecca Flashyfur. "That coldhearted cavemouse is deliberately excluding me from the contest!"

Her mother answered her with **glacial** calm. "Don't worry, darling, I'll take care of it." She found it impossible to say **no** to her daughter. "I'll call the professor. What did you say his name was again?"

"Cavemou—I mean, **Bruce Hyena**!"

A GIFT WITH STRINGS ATTACHED

Bruce was new to the world of teaching, so when he received a call from *Rebecca Flashyfur*, he didn't know what to do. He'd never squeaked with such a **pushypaws** parent before! He got as nervous and confused as a lab rat in a maze.

"Ah-ahem, y-yes, madam . . . I-I'm Professor Hyena!" he stammered.

Those were the last words to leave his snout. After that, he was struck **squeakless** while Mrs. Flashyfur showered him with compliments.

"My darling mouselings have spoken so highly of you. Your course is so **INNOVATIVE**. It seems only right I should support it with a donation," she sighed. Then she got in her final **ZING**. "I'll donate a new sailboat to the academy. These hardworking students have earned nothing less than the *NEWEST* model! If we work together, Mouseford is guaranteed to win the *prestigious* Rodents' Regatta!"

"MOLDY MOZZARELLA!"

Ooops!

Bruce was so astonished, the phone slid out of his paw like a slippery slice of Swiss. When he picked it up again, Rebecca Flashyfur was still *SQUEAKING*.

"And of course, in exchange, you'll let my dear

mouselings Ryder and Ruby participate in the survival CONTEST!"

After that, the line went dead. Bruce shook his snout, trying to SNAP out of his stupor.

"Now I know where Ruby learned all her tricks!" he GROANED. "I can't believe her mother is willing to donate a new sailboat to the academy just to get her mouselings into the contest!"

Bruce's tail was twisting with outrage. He would never give in to blackmail. NEVER! He grabbed the **list** of contestants and headed toward the door.

Suddenly, he had an idea. He grinned. "The time has come to teach that spoiled little cheese puff an **important** lesson!"

Bruce had a plan. If all went well, the contest could be just the thing to teach Ruby the importance of **RESPECT** — not just for nature, but for other rodents, too.

"I'll find a way to squeeze her and her brother into the contest. This could end up being a good experience for all of them, or my name isn't **BRUCE HYENA**!"

SURPRISE PAIRS!

When the contestants read the final participant list on the school BULLETIN BOARD, they were horrified. All the pairs had been MIXED UP!

Bruce had added Ruby and Ryder to the original list of twelve. Then he'd programmed his **COMPUTER** to randomly select the seven pairs. This was the result:

TEAMS:
Pamela/Tanja   Colette/Shen
Craig/Zoe   Alicia/Violet
Nicky/Elly   Ruby/Sebastian

SPECIAL TEAM:
Paulina/Ryder

Exclamations of amazement filled the room. The new teams had taken everyone by Surprise.

Zoe jumped for JOY when she saw that her new partner was Craig. And Sebastian, who'd had a crush on Ruby since the beginning of the year, couldn't take his EYES off his name next to hers.

But Colette was disappointed. "Now that we aren't together, the contest won't be any fun," she told Pam.

"I've got it *way* worse than you, Colette," said Violet. "My new partner is Alicia, and she's totally out to get me!"

"Don't you guys see?" interrupted Nicky. She was LOYAL to her teacher. "Professor Hyena did it on purpose! Switching up partners is the first part of the test. Remember what he told us?

"THE MOST IMPORTANT PART OF SURVIVAL IS ADAPTING TO UNFORESEEN ELEMENTS!""

Colette frowned at her. "Easy for you to say—you and Elly are going to be a **GREAT** team!"

"But what about me?" asked Paulina, a little **bewildered**. "Look! It says 'Special Team: Ryder and Paulina'! What do you think that means?"

The most **SURPRISED** mouse of all was Ryder. He hadn't even signed up! Paulina scanned the crowd until she spotted him. He was in a heated discussion with his sister. That's when Paulina realized the new teams had Ruby's **PAWS** all over them.

"Don't you get it, Ryder? They gave in like

always!" she was boasting to her brother. "With this contest, I'll show everybody that the Flashyfurs always come out on top! I already have the perfect plan. The Thea Sisters will be left behind like yesterday's **cheese rinds**, and I'll win without even ruffling my fur. So much for that cavemouse's useless lessons!"

Ryder just shrugged. He knew that when Ruby got an IDEA stuck in her head, there was nothing anyone could do to change her mind. Besides, the contest seemed like it might be cool.

THE CONTEST RULES

The seven pairs gathered in the gym. They found Professor Hyena busy with his afternoon exercises: one hundred push-ups on each paw!

"Ninety-eight . . . ninety nine . . . one hundred!"

Hup, hup, hup!

As soon as everyone had settled down, Bruce pawed each pair a map of the island.

"Listen up, cheese puffs, the fun is about to begin! Six pairs will be taken to the Forest of Hawks and left in six different places," he explained. "Don't try to **contact** one another, understand?"

Then he pulled out a backpack he'd prepared.

"Every pair will have a kit like this one, with all the essential equipment," Professor Hyena told the students. "Don't take anything else with you. As soon as you arrive, start building a SHELTER and finding food and DRINK. And remember, you must work together to deal with all your needs — and that includes needs you may not anticipate!"

A shovel?

Here's your gear!

"What if something goes wrong?" Tanja asked anxiously. "What if there's **DANGER**?"

Bruce took a minuscule **BLACK** device from the backpack.

"There's a GPS beacon in the kit," he explained. "Press the **red** button, and a rescue team will come pick you up, day or night," He paused and gave them a **STERN** look. "But let me be clear. When one team member presses the button, the pair is *disqualified* from the contest!"

Ruby jumped up as if a cat had stepped on her **TAIL**. "That's not fair! You shouldn't lose just because your partner is a **CHEESEBRAIN**!" She cast a dirty look at Sebastian, who lowered his eyes *sadly*.

Bruce put a comforting paw on Sebastian's

shoulders. "You're starting off on the wrong paw, little cheese puff," he told Ruby. "You'll be surprised how much you can learn from others in an experience like this—

and how amazing it can be to share an **ADVENTURE** with a true friend!"

Relieved, Sebastian gave the professor a big GRIN. Ruby just yawned.

Bruce turned back to the group. "Everybody, get this through your fur. This contest is nothing to sneeze at! The goal is to learn how to work together in **DIFFICULT** situations. That's why a pair will win, not a single mouseling!"

"Exactly how long is the contest?" asked Pamela.

"From dawn on Saturday until dusk on Sunday," answered Bruce. He took off his mirrored SUNGLASSES and stared down each student, one by one. "I will be the judge of which pair best displays their survival skills, and my judgment will be final!"

On that note, the group broke up and headed to their rooms to get ready.

Paulina was confused. Professor Hyena hadn't said a word about the "special team" or her role in it. She was about to approach him when he grinned at her and said, "Paulina, Ryder—hang on a second! I have a few things to explain."

Ryder had stayed in the corner of the gym for Bruce's whole speech. He was pretending he didn't CARE about the contest. Actually, he was more *curious* than a cat about what the professor had organized. Ryder hadn't taken the survival class, but he **liked** the eccentric teacher and had a feeling he'd see some interesting things during the contest.

A SPECIAL mission

Professor Hyena waited until everyone was gone. Then he pulled out the keys to a Jeep.

"You two will take the pairs to their designated places," he began.

"That's it?" Ryder asked, surprised. "The only thing we have to do is be chauffeurs? Some SPECIAL assignment!"

Even Paulina was surprised, though she tried to HIDE it.

"Can we go now?" Ryder asked, his disappointment showing.

"Negative!" Bruce answered. "I haven't told you the best part yet! Aren't you my special team?"

"What exactly does that mean?" blurted

Paulina. She couldn't contain her **CURIOSITY** a moment longer.

Bruce laughed. "I've reserved the best job for you two champs. I swear it on a stack of cheese slices!" He gave them two fancy **cameras**.

"Here's your assignment," Professor Hyena explained. "You will be my eyes and ears during the competition! You must observe

These are for you!

the contestants secretly and capture their most interesting moments. You will be the competition's official **PHOTOGRAPHERS**."

Paulina was thrilled. "cheesecake! I love photojournalism!"

Ryder grinned. "Sounds more like **spying** than photojournalism, but that's cool."

Bruce winked at him. "To get from one place to another, you'll use the **JEEP**," he continued. "But you have to approach the contestants by paw, very stealthily, so they never know you're there. That's the only way your **PHOTOS** will capture the true spirit of the competition." He lowered his squeak and added, "Here's your strategy: *sleek* but *silent*, like mice in rice!"

An AWESOME ADVENTURE

That night, the academy's two clubs—the LIZARDS (the club for girl mice) and the GECKOS (the club for boy mice)—convened to discuss the survival contest. Everyone was buzzing about who would be the first to GIVE UP, who would stick it out to the end, and most importantly, who would WIN!

Small groups began to form in support of one team or another. The most numerous—and the most noisy—were Craig's female fans, who gazed enviously at the LUCKY Zoe.

Less numerous but just as enthusiastic were Nicky's and Elly's fans, who were sure

the two mouselets were guaranteed to win.

Also present were Ruby's not-so-secret admirers, who'd hung **BIG BANNERS** in her honor.

After chatting and sharing tea with the other mice, The Thea Sisters left the Lizards' gathering early. They had to be up at dawn the next morning, and they wanted to get a good night's sleep.

Pamela hugged Colette. "I'm sorry, Colette! I promised you we'd be in the contest together . . ."

"I'm DISAPPOINTED, but it's okay," Colette reassured her. "I think this contest is going to be full of surprises, and you know me—I *love* surprises!"

"It's going to be an awesome *adventure*," said Nicky.

Paulina smiled and stretched out her paw.

Pamela immediately put her paw on top of her friend's, and the others joined in, too.

"MORE THAN FRIENDS, SISTERS! THE THEA SISTERS!"

THE PERFECT OUTFIT?!

Zoe was the happiest of all the contestants. Getting Craig as her partner was a **stroke of pure luck**! The mouselet didn't shut her eyes all night. She couldn't stop thinking

about all the time she was going to spend one-on-one with Craig! By the end of the weekend, they were sure to be the **BEST** of friends.

"Just think of all the time we'll have to **laugh** and talk," she sighed. "I'll finally have him all to myself!" She couldn't wait until dawn.

It took Zoe a long time to pick out the right **CLOTHES** to wear to impress Craig. She reviewed dozens of outfits and **REJECTED** them all. Finally, she selected a SHINY skirt, a fuchsia top, a pair of purple ballet flats, and lots of sparkly bracelets.

When the time came to meet up with the other contestants, the moon was still SHINING in the sky. Zoe's clothes shimmered under the silvery rays, like she'd just stepped under a *disco ball*! She smiled radiantly.

Craig paused to look at his partner from snout to tail. He was **SURPRISED** by her choice of clothing. It was so

I have nothing to wear!

unsuitable for a survival competition in the woods!

"Slimy Swiss rolls!"

he exclaimed, shaking his snout. What was she thinking?

Zoe shot him a satisfied smile. She was sure he was already under her **spell**!

THE CHALLENGE BEGINS!

A little before dawn, Paulina and Ryder escorted the teams to locations Professor Hyena had marked on their **MaP**. Then they dedicated themselves to the second part of their mission: **THE SECRET PHOTO SHOOT**!

During class, Bruce had explained that the first thing a camper must do is decide where to build **SHELTER**, and then look in the woods for food and **water**. But once all the teams arrived in their sections of the forest, each interpreted this advice differently. . . .

Craig didn't waste time looking around for the **BEST** place to build a shelter. He just grabbed an ax and began Chopping down trees and bushes.

"Don't just sit there. Give me a paw!" he told Zoe, who was leaning dreamily against a tree. "Clean the branches and divide the **THICK** ones from the *THIN* ones."

Zoe stared at him. She didn't have a clue what he meant. "Clean the branches?" she repeated.

"Take off the leaves! Make them *smooth*!" he answered. He continued striking his ax without bothering to look at her.

Reluctantly, Zoe obeyed. This was certainly not the way she'd pictured spending time with the mouse of her **dreams**!

Meanwhile, Tanja and Pamela were studying the entire territory they'd been assigned. The area was rich with bushes and **berries**.

Tanja was a bit of an expert on edible **plants**. "My grandmother lives in the mountains and taught me how to recognize them," she explained. "See this plant? It's called pokeweed, and it's very poisonous. But if we cook the young shoots, we can eat them."

Pokeweed

"*Fabumouse*!" exclaimed Pamela. "I don't suppose your grandmother taught you a good recipe?"

"Actually, my family is full of real FOODIES!" said Tanja, winking.

It turned out the two mouselets shared a passion for good Food. They immediately began hunting for berries and EDIBLE mushrooms.

Pam and Tanja seemed to go together like bagels and cream cheese. After a couple of hours, they found themselves far from the starting point, so they stopped at a SPRING to quench their thirst and wash the fruit they'd gathered.

"Now we need **fire**," said Tanja.

"And shelter," replied Pamela.

Luck was on their side. Right there, two feet from the **SPRING**, they discovered a cave that was small but cozy. It was the perfect place to spend the night!

CAT-ASTROPHIC COMBINATIONS!

As for Alicia and Violet—well, they were more like pickles and whipped cream than bagels and cream cheese. Violet was quiet and thoughtful, and she hated gossip and rumors. As for Alicia, well . . . she squeaked CONSTANTLY, even in her sleep!

Their personalities were as different as cheddar and Swiss. IT WAS A CAT-ASTROPHIC COMBINATION!

As Alicia chatted away, Violet tried to get a squeak in edgewise. "Why don't we quiet down for a second, please, so we can hear the sounds of the woods?"

Alicia opened her eyes wide in surprise.

"The SOUNDS of the woods? Hmm,

yes, you're right, of course," Alicia babbled. "The woods are full of sounds . . . in fact, it reminds me of that **MOVIE**! Now, what's it called again? Oh yeah, *Spooks in the Snowstorm*. **HOLEY CHEESE**, how I loved it! Robert Rattinson, the leading mouse, is my favorite actor! Did you see him in *The Porcupine*?"

Violet tried to tune her out, but Alicia's prattle PIERCED her brain. Violet could hardly hear herself think. Didn't her teammate ever need to catch her breath?

Alicia continued squeaking all morning and afternoon, until . . .

"**ENOUGH!**" shouted Violet in exasperation.

Surprised, Alicia fell silent at last.

Violet took a deep breath.

"Listen, why don't we *divide up* our

tasks?" Violet suggested. "You go search for food and I'll look for shelter, okay?" Violet climbed up on a high, flat ROCK so she could get a better look around. There, immersed in the peaceful sounds and sights of the woods, she finally calmed down. For the first time since she and Alicia had left the academy, she was able to relax.

In the meantime, Colette was **bored** stiff. The idea of the competition had never really appealed to her, and the thought of being in the woods for two whole days without her best friends and her favorite SUITCASE made her grumpier than a mouse in a maze.

As if that weren't bad enough, she found herself with Shen, who did nothing but talk about Pam. His crush on her friend was LEGENDARY.

"Pamela is such an awesome mouselet!" he kept saying. "I'm sure she'll win the contest! She'll build a FABUMOUSE shelter."

Fortunately, after a couple hours' exploration, Colette found a delightful distraction.

"A waterfall!" she exclaimed, scampering toward the clear, *sparkling* water falling from the side of a rock. "I knew wearing a **_bathing suit_** under my clothes was a good idea! I'm going for a swim!"

Shen shook his snout. Then he started building a shelter for the night while Colette frolicked in the **fresh** water.

MARVEMOUSE MATCHES

Nicky and Elly were by far the best matched team. They were good friends who were excited about **working together**. And both had followed Bruce's lessons closely.

"We have to find a **dry** place," said Nicky.

"But it needs to be near **WATER**, so we can prepare our meals," Elly added.

The two friends shared a love of the outdoors, so for them, building shelter and making camp was more **fun** than a trip to the New Mouse City Cheese Fest.

Nicky and Elly shared Bruce's motto: Respect nature, and use whatever she gives you to your best advantage! To build their shelter, they used **STONES** and the

BRANCHES that had fallen to the ground. Then they chose a protected spot close to a large boulder, and used poles and a **rope** tied between two trees to support the waterproof cloth for their hut. Finally, they fastened the CANVAS to the ground with stakes anchored by large rocks.

Beneath the tent, the two mouselets created a carpet of twigs so they wouldn't have to sleep directly on the **damp** ground. A few feet in front of the shelter's opening, they arranged stones in a circle and built a **fire**.

"This turned out great!" said Elly with **SATISFACTION**.

Nicky agreed. "The only thing left to do is look for food," she added.

Not too far away from them, Ruby and Sebastian were getting along, which was certainly **unexpected**. But it wouldn't be fair to say they collaborated!

From the moment Paulina and Ryder dropped them off, Sebastian did everything he could to make sure his companion didn't have to lift a paw.

"You just sit there and **DON'T WORRY** about a thing," he said. "I'll take care of you!"

Ruby smiled at him sweetly. "Sebastian, if you can keep a teensy $secret$, you won't have to move another muscle!"

You see, Ruby had come up with a detailed **survival plan**. She had no intention of following Bruce's instructions. Instead, she put her faith in technology!

With the aid of a powerful transceiver, her personal assistant, Alan, could identify Ruby's location and bring her everything she needed: an inflatable tent, food, **MAKEUP**, and even video games.

"Winning this competition is going to be easier than taking cheese from a mouseling!" Ruby WHISPERED to Sebastian.

And that's how I'll win the competition!

THE CHEESY SMELL OF DECEPTION

The SUN was already low on the horizon when Alan, Ruby's assistant, arrived in the forest. Under the thick tree branches, it was growing **darker** and gloomier, but Ruby had made Alan promise to drive with his headlights off so he wouldn't be spotted.

As he *sped* along in the twilight, Alan didn't notice a large branch in the middle of the road. His Jeep crashed right over it.

CRASH!

The Jeep gave a sudden lurch, and a can of CHEESY CHEWS flew out of a box in the back. It rolled and rolled until it stopped underneath a big BUSH.

Alan didn't notice that he'd lost some of

his cargo. His Jeep kept bumping along, leaving clouds of dust in its wake.

Half an hour later, Shen happened upon the exact spot Alan had passed. He'd ventured into the underbrush to look for **eDiBLe** berries while Colette enjoyed the waterfall.

Shen was so absorbed in the interesting *plants* around him, he didn't notice he'd drifted farther and farther from the campsite. Suddenly he looked up and realized it was dark. He turned on his **flashlight** and began retracing his steps.

The flashlight's beam illuminated a **THICK** bush. Something glinted from underneath its branches. *Intrigued*, Shen moved closer.

"What is this?" he wondered. He bent over to pick it up.

"CHEESY CHEWS?" Shen said in surprise. Then he slipped the can into his backpack.

Shen went to find Colette at the campsite. He proudly showed her the **herbs** and **berries** he'd gathered. He knew each by its scientific name and property. Colette looked at them uncertainly, and then timidly took a berry and tasted it.

"**YUCK!** It's bitter!" she protested, grimacing.

"It's rich in *Vitamin C,*" Shen told her. "Let's have a big serving of these for dinner,

and we'll go to sleep with nice, full bellies."

Colette wrinkled her snout. Her expression made Shen remember the can he'd found.

"Well, there's also this. . . ."

"A can of **CHEESY CHEWS**? Where'd you get it?" asked Colette **suspiciously**.

"I found it underneath a bush by the road. **Strange**, right?"

Colette frowned and sniffed the air. "Do

you smell that, Shen?"

Shen sniffed, too, and then shrugged. "Nope, I don't smell anything."

"IT'S THE CHEESY SMELL OF DECEPTION,"

Colette declared. "One of the other teams is up to no good. And I have a feeling I know which one. . . ."

SURPRISE FROM THE SKY

Paulina and Ryder were surprised to find themselves **ENJOYING** their stealth mission. They'd *raced* from one end of the forest to the other, and had captured their friends' struggle with nature in dozens of photos. But now **NIGHT** was falling, and they were returning to the academy in their Jeep.

"Look at this funny FACE Pamela's making! And Sebastian—he stubbed his toe in this one!" Paulina said, looking through pictures on her camera's screen.

"This has been a really fun day," admitted Ryder. "But I keep finding leaves

and twigs stuck in my fur. Going undercover is no day at the cheese shop! **Ha, Ha, Ha!**"

Paulina giggled as she plucked a twig from behind his ear. "You look a little funny, I have to admit. But what about me? Remember how I almost fell out of that tree and onto Shen's tail? **Ha, Ha, Ha!**"

The two mice had a good chuckle over that one. But as soon as their laughter died down, they heard a sound: **DRIP!**

And then again:

The sound grew more insistent. A moment later, the Jeep's windshield was covered with raindrops as big as mozzarella balls.

Lightning ripped through the sky, followed by a loud thunderclap.

KABooM!

On Whale Island, the weather could change in an instant. In springtime, **DOWNPOURS** often came quite suddenly!

In the space of a minute, the endurance competition had become **HARDER** than a block of petrified cheddar. This sudden rainstorm was a lot more than the six teams had bargained for. . . .

SOS! SOS!

The wooden frame and tent that Craig had built was solid and completely *waterproof*. No rain or wind could penetrate it. If he and Zoe stayed inside, they were guaranteed to be **WARM** and cozy. But they hadn't looked for any food, and their stomachs were emptier than a candy store the day after Halloween.

"I **BROKE** two pawnails!" Zoe COMPLAINED. "Plus I ripped my skirt and twisted an ankle!"

"I'm not sure how you broke those nails, because you hardly lifted a Paw to help me," Craig said, rolling his eyes. "It took you all day to find two mushrooms and a couple of wild berries!"

Zoe's snout turned PALE. Craig was disappointed in her? She hadn't realized

that. His disapproval was the last thing she wanted.

Craig saw the shocked look on her snout. "**WHAT DUMB LUCK!** Of all the rodents in this competition, I got stuck with Miss Clueless," he muttered.

All Zoe's *romantic* fantasies crumbled like a house of cheese crackers. *What a jerk,*

she thought. *How dare he treat me like a dumb cheese puff! Well, I'll show him. I'm going back to school!*

She grabbed the backpack, pulled out the GPS beacon, and pressed the red button.

BEEEEP!

Bruce's search party immediately picked up the signal and hurried to rescue Craig and Zoe. For them, the competition was **OVER**!

A very different fate awaited Shen and Colette. Their shelter was not as well grounded as Craig's. And unfortunately, they'd placed it very close to the small stream that flowed into the waterfall.

The **DOWNPOUR** quickly transformed the stream's trickle into a swirling torrent that swept away the fragile hut.

CRAAAAASH!

When the swollen stream hit them, Shen clung to a TREE and managed to stay afloat. But Colette had been snug inside her sleeping bag, and the zipper got STUCK. She couldn't get out! The current dragged her away.

"HEEEEELP!"

Colette shrieked at the top of her lungs.

Shen heard her screams and spotted the bright orange sleeping bag drifting down the stream. Bravely, he hurried into the water after her. He almost fell a few times, but at last he managed to grab the sleeping bag.

Using all his might, Shen tugged it out of the raging stream and tied the water-soaked **BUNDLE** to a tree. Once his paws were free,

he yanked the stuck zipper and opened it.

Colette burst out of the sleeping bag like a **moth** freed from its cocoon. She threw her paws around Shen's neck in a great **BIG HUG.**♥♥♥

Once they'd recovered, Colette and Shen considered their situation. They were soaked to the fur, their shelter was gone, and they had no fire to dry themselves. So they decided to press the red button.

BEEEEP!

EVERYONE
TAKES SHELTER!

Meanwhile, Pamela and Tanja were warm
and dry inside their little CAVE. Tanja had
roasted the roots, berries, and even some of
the flowers they'd picked. The two mouselets
had cooked up a tasty dinner!

"Mmm, that hit the spot," said Pam,
rubbing her belly. "And we're so lucky to be
safe and dry in here. Check out the weather
outside." She turned her ear toward the cave
opening. "Listen to that WIND blow! It
sounds like a WOLF howling."

Tanja walked to the cave's mouth and
peered out. "Um, Pam? I think it IS
howling! There's someone screaming out
there!"

Tanja was right. It was Violet and Alicia, **SCREAMING** at each other!

"You dropped our backpacks in a ditch! Now how are we going to send out the **SIGNAL** for Professor Hyena to come get us?" complained Violet.

"It's your fault!" Alicia shot back. "Instead of thinking about shelter, you sat on your tail and **MEDITATED**!"

Who's howling out there?

Pamela scurried toward them. "What are you two doing out here in the **rain**?" she asked. Without waiting for an answer, she

herded them toward the cave. "Come with me!"

Violet's and Alicia's fur was soaked through. They took one look at the warm, inviting shelter that Pam and Tanja had found, and all their bitterness vanished in an instant. They hurried inside.

Tanja offered them a flask. "Go ahead, drink! It's hot **HERBAL TEA**."

Alicia could feel her tail warming up again.

"Mmm, it's delicious!"

"Thanks for sharing your shelter with us, Pam," Violet said. "But isn't it against the rules for us to pair up? If you take us in, you'll be **disqualified**!"

Pam **shrugged**. "So what? It's no big deal."

"Helping friends is way more *important* than winning a competition," agreed Tanja.

Violet **BEAMED** at them. "Friends like you two are worth your weight in cheese!"

You're such a good friend!

RELiEF in ACTion

Meanwhile, Ryder and Paulina were just pulling through Mouseford Academy's main gates. They ran into Professor Hyena, who was **HURRYING** to answer the **EMERGENCY SIGNALS**. He'd organized a fleet of emergency vehicles to pick up the competitors who were in **TROUBLE**.

"Someone withdrew from the competition?" Ryder asked.

Bruce nodded. "Affirmative! The very first was none other than your friend the sportsmouse, Craig." Then he rushed off.

Paulina stared after him, feeling worried. Her friends were in the woods in that **foul weather**! Ryder was trying not to show it, but she could tell that deep down, he was anxious about his sister.

"We should go with him," Paulina suggested. "I want to **make sure** everyone's okay."

"Well, all right, if you really want to. I guess I could take a few photos of the storm," agreed Ryder, **playing** it cool as a cat.

Paulina smiled. She'd noticed he had the Jeep's keys ready in his paws.

The Jeep roared away. About twenty minutes later, Paulina and Ryder had arrived at Nicky and Elly's **TENT**. Even from a distance, they could see it was sturdy and protected from the **WIND**.

"Nothing to **worry** about when it comes to Nicky," said Paulina.

Next Paulina and Ryder went to check on Violet and Alicia, but found **NOTHING** at their campsite — no sign of shelter, or of the **TWO** mouselets.

"They must have bailed," said Ryder.

But Paulina shook her snout. She wasn't so sure about that.

"Let's go see Pam," Ryder suggested. "She's in that **CAVE** nearby. Maybe she knows something."

As they drew closer to Pam and Tanja's shelter, they heard the sound of several **squeaks** raised in song. They were a bit off key, and the squeaking ended in a roar of **LAUGHTER**.

"Ha! Ha! Ha! Ha! Ha! Ha!"

Paulina would recognize Violet's laugh anywhere. She was so dumbfounded, she couldn't help herself. She **RAN** inside the cave.

"Violet? Pamela? Alicia? Tanja?" she exclaimed.

Ryder was at her heels. He grinned when he saw the four mouselets. "Looks like you've turned the survival competition into a **PAJAMA PARTY**!"

Pam, Violet, Alicia, and Tanja greeted their friends enthusiastically. Tanja offered them some of the food she'd cooked.

"Why don't you stay with them?" Ryder whispered to Paulina. "I want to shoot a few more *photos*."

The truth was, he wanted to make sure his

sister was okay. But as soon as he spotted the enormouse **INFLATABLE** tent, he knew that as usual, Ruby had found the easiest way to win.

"Sis, you are hopeless!"

he whispered, shaking his snout.

GRRR . . . I'M SO EMBARRASSED!

Ryder was about to head back to the Jeep when a bolt of lightning lit up the woods.

CRAAACK!

A branch snapped off a tree. It landed right on Ruby's inflatable tent, puncturing it.

THUMP . . . PSHHHHHHHH!

The tent sagged as air leaked out of it. Sebastian and Ruby DASHED OUT just moments before it collapsed.

As Ruby scurried along in her long bathrobe, she slid in the mud and fell flat on her snout! PLUNK!

Ryder grinned. He couldn't resist such a perfect photo opportunity. FLASH!

The next morning, all the mouselets met back at Mouseford Academy.

"The CONTEST is over," Professor Hyena declared. "And I'm proud to announce our winners: Nicky and Elly!" He grinned as the other students cheered. "These two mouselets have proved themselves master-mice of **survival**! I'd trust their instincts in any situation."

Bruce also had praise for another team. "A special survival shout-out goes to two mice who helped their buddies when they were in trouble. Pam and Tanja, you understand the true meaning of friendship!"

As for Ruby, she stayed in bed for the rest of the day. She locked the door and put a MASK over her eyes. The contest had been a complete disaster, and she was sure she was having a NERVOUS BREAKDOWN!

Ruby and Sebastian had pressed the emergency button—but not before hiding the **deflated** tent. Ruby's assistant had removed all the other incriminating evidence.

Professor Hyena never discovered that she had **CHEATED**. But Ruby had been forced

to return to Mouseford covered in mud from snout to paw, and that was humiliation enough.

"Grrr . . . I'm so embarrassed!"

The mud had irritated her delicate fur, so now she was covered with little red spots.

"Grrr . . . I'm absolutely mortified!"

But the worst part was that thanks to Nicky's victory, Pamela's good heart, and Paulina's awesome photojournalism, the Thea Sisters were the stars of the show . . . again.

"Grrr . . . I'm madder than a mouse stuck in a glue trap!"

Little did Ruby realize that her problems were just beginning. . . .

A MAGAZINE JUST ABOUT US!

The next week, all the students who'd competed in the survival contest wrote essays about their EXPERiENCE. Next to each piece was a photograph capturing the competition's **HIGHS** and **LOWS**.

Headmaster Octavius de Mousus asked the editor of the magazine *Top Trips* to read all the students' essays. They were so entertaining, and Paulina and Ryder's photos so terrific, that she decided to publish all of them in a **special issue** dedicated to camping.

On the last day of Professor Hyena's survival course, every student received a copy of the magazine at a ceremony held in the auditorium.

Ruby showed up in a hat and a veil to cover the sulk on her snout. She'd been *thrilled* when she heard she was on the magazine's front cover. But her excitement quickly turned to fury when she saw the actual picture. It showed her running in a frumpy bathrobe, covered with **MUD** from snout to tail! Above the picture was the headline: *Camping Dos and Don'ts: The Top Ten Things Never to Do in the Woods!*

The headmaster began to squeak.

"Students, Professor Hyena and I are very **PROUD** of you! You've had a priceless experience, and you've **learned** the importance of collaboration in a paws-on way. Because this course has been such a *success*, I've decided to invite Professor Hyena back next year for another *special* lecture series!"

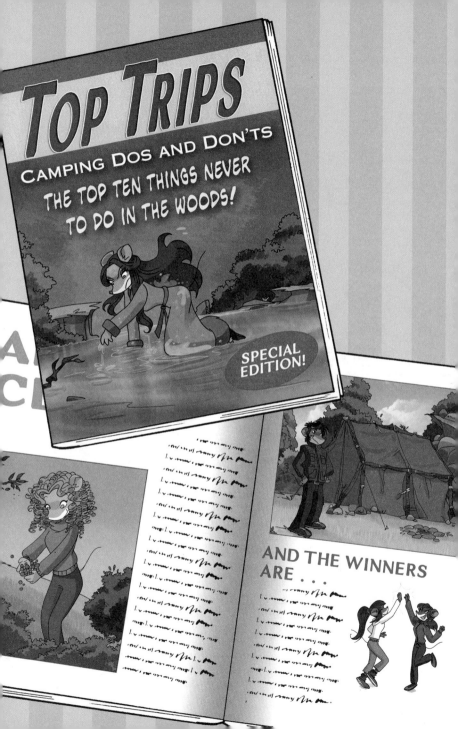

The classroom broke into thunderous applause.

CLAP! CLAP! CLAP!

Colette took Professor Hyena aside for a second and whispered, "Professor, were you able to solve the mystery of the can of CHEESY CHEWS?"

Bravo, mouselings!

"No, I never found any proof," he answered, glancing at Ruby. "But the SPOILED LITTLE CHEESE PUFF who tried to cheat during the competition sure got what was coming to her, and that's nothing to sneeze at!

She's lucky to have me around to teach her, or my name isn't Bruce Hyena!"

Don't miss any of these Mouseford Academy adventures!

#1 Drama at Mouseford

#2 The Missing Diary

#3 Mouselets in Danger

#4 Dance Challenge

#5 The Secret Invention

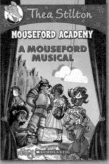

#6 A Mouseford Musical

Don't miss these exciting Thea Sisters adventures!

Thea Stilton and the
Dragon's Code

Thea Stilton and the
Mountain of Fire

Thea Stilton and the
Ghost of the Shipwreck

Thea Stilton and the
Secret City

Thea Stilton and the
Mystery in Paris

Thea Stilton and the
Cherry Blossom Adventure

Thea Stilton and the
Star Castaways

Thea Stilton: Big Trouble
in the Big Apple

Thea Stilton and the
Ice Treasure

Thea Stilton and the
Secret of the Old Castle

Thea Stilton and the
Blue Scarab Hunt

Thea Stilton and the
Prince's Emerald

Thea Stilton and the Mystery
on the Orient Express

Thea Stilton and the
Dancing Shadows

Thea Stilton and the
Legend of the Fire Flowers

Thea Stilton and the
Spanish Dance Mission

Thea Stilton and the
Journey to the Lion's Den

Thea Stilton and the
Great Tulip Heist

Thea Stilton and the
Chocolate Sabotage

Thea Stilton and the
Missing Myth

Check out these very special editions featuring me and the Thea Sisters!

THE JOURNEY TO ATLANTIS

THE SECRET OF THE FAIRIES

THE SECRET OF THE SNOW

Be sure to read all my fabumouse adventures!

#1 Lost Treasure of the Emerald Eye

#2 The Curse of the Cheese Pyramid

#3 Cat and Mouse in a Haunted House

#4 I'm Too Fond of My Fur!

#5 Four Mice Deep in the Jungle

#6 Paws Off, Cheddarface!

#7 Red Pizzas for a Blue Count

#8 Attack of the Bandit Cats

#9 A Fabumouse Vacation for Geronimo

#10 All Because of a Cup of Coffee

#11 It's Halloween, You 'Fraidy Mouse!

#12 Merry Christmas, Geronimo!

#13 The Phantom of the Subway

#14 The Temple of the Ruby of Fire

#15 The Mona Mousa Code

#16 A Cheese-Colored Camper

#17 Watch Your Whiskers, Stilton!

#18 Shipwreck on the Pirate Islands

#19 My Name Is Stilton, Geronimo Stilton

#20 Surf's Up, Geronimo!

#21 The Wild, Wild West

#22 The Secret of Cacklefur Castle

A Christmas Tale

#23 Valentine's Day Disaster

#24 Field Trip to Niagara Falls

#25 The Search for Sunken Treasure

#26 The Mummy with No Name

#27 The Christmas Toy Factory

#28 Wedding Crasher

#29 Down and Out Down Under

#30 The Mouse Island Marathon

#31 The Mysterious Cheese Thief

Christmas Catastrophe

#32 Valley of the Giant Skeletons

#33 Geronimo and the Gold Medal Mystery

#34 Geronimo Stilton, Secret Agent

#35 A Very Merry Christmas

#36 Geronimo's Valentine

#37 The Race Across America

#38 A Fabumouse School Adventure

#39 Singing Sensation

#40 The Karate Mouse

#41 Mighty Mount Kilimanjaro

#42 The Peculiar Pumpkin Thief

#43 I'm Not a Supermouse!

#44 The Giant Diamond Robbery

#45 Save the White Whale!

#46 The Haunted Castle

#47 Run for the Hills, Geronimo!

#48 The Mystery in Venice

#49 The Way of the Samurai

#50 This Hotel Is Haunted!

#51 The Enormouse Pearl Heist

#52 Mouse in Space!

#53 Rumble in the Jungle

#54 Get into Gear, Stilton!

#55 The Golden Statue Plot

#56 Flight of the Red Bandit

The Hunt for the Golden Book

#57 The Stinky Cheese Vacation

#58 The Super Chef Contest

#59 Welcome to Moldy Manor

Don't miss my journey through time!

THE JOURNEY THROUGH TIME

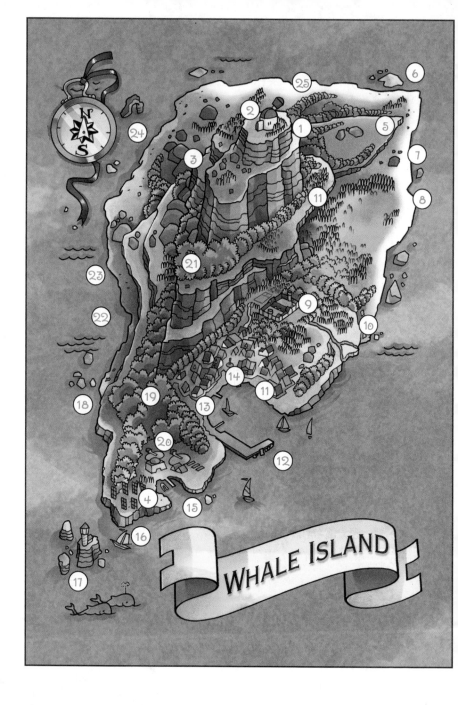

WHALE ISLAND

MAP OF WHALE ISLAND

1. Falcon Peak
2. Observatory
3. Mount Landslide
4. Solar Energy Plant
5. Ram Plain
6. Very Windy Point
7. Turtle Beach
8. Beachy Beach
9. Mouseford Academy
10. Kneecap River
11. Mariner's Inn
12. Port
13. Squid House
14. Town Square
15. Butterfly Bay
16. Mussel Point
17. Lighthouse Cliff
18. Pelican Cliff
19. Nightingale Woods
20. Marine Biology Lab
21. Hawk Woods
22. Windy Grotto
23. Seal Grotto
24. Seagulls Bay
25. Seashell Beach

THANKS FOR READING,
AND GOOD-BYE UNTIL OUR
NEXT MOUSEFORD
ADVENTURE!

TheaSisters